Mungo
and the
Picture Book
PIRATES

TIMOTHY KNAPMAN AND ADAM STOWER

PUFFIN

MUNGO'S ROOM

KEEP OUT!

PUFFIN BOOKS

Published by the Penguin Group: London, New York, Australia,
Canada, India, Ireland, New Zealand and South Africa
Penguin Books Ltd, Registered Offices:
80 Strand, London WC2R 0RL, England

puffinbooks.com

First published 2005
011
Published in this edition 2006
Text copyright © Timothy Knapman, 2005
Illustrations copyright © Adam Stower, 2005
All rights reserved
The moral right of the author and illustrator has been asserted
Made and printed in China
ISBN: 978–0–140–56974–2

To Freddy, Tom and Joe
(who gave me the idea in the first place)
with love – T.K.

For Bill & Norah,
and plucky Zoë
with love – A.S.

This is **Mungo**.

His favourite book is called

The Seafaring Adventures of Captain Horatio Fleet.

Last thing **every** night,
he makes his mum read it to him.

Twice if she's lucky.

FIVE TIMES
if she's not!

And this is how the
story goes . . .

Nora and Admiral Mainbrace

Once upon a time, Admiral Mainbrace and his **PLUCKY** cabin girl, Nora, set sail in their fine Spanish galleon.

They had **only** been at sea for two days when they were **attacked** by **Barnacle Bill**, the terror of the high seas! (And his dreaded purple berserker bird!)

Barnacle Bill

Barnacle Bill's crew of scurvy pirates **fell** upon the Admiral's galleon in a flashing of cutlasses.

They **plundered** its treasure and **looted** its booty!

But, most frightening by far,
they sang sea shanties so foul
that anyone who heard them
begged
to walk
the plank.

It would all have ended badly for
Admiral Mainbrace and Nora if their cries for
help hadn't been heard by . . .

Captain Horatio Fleet, the bravest
ship's captain of them all!

DARING
Captain Fleet,
who **defeated** the dreaded
Octopus of Bognor!

Bognor, 1709

DASHING
Captain Fleet,
who **juggled** with
sharks and electric eels!

Port Royal, 1711

Blackbeard's Cafe, 1712

DAZZLING
Captain Fleet,
who ate piranha fish fingers
and chips for his tea!

He swung to the rescue at once!

"Not so fast, you scurvy dogs!" cried Captain Fleet
as he unplundered the treasure and de-looted the booty.
Then he tied the villains' throats in an expert
display of knots so that they could
never sing sea shanties again.

"Hooray!" cried the Admiral.
"We're saved!"
And Captain Fleet married that
PLUCKY cabin girl, Nora.

Together they set sail for the sinking sun, and all the adventures that wait in the waters off the coast of tomorrow.

The End

"Again, Mummy! Read it again!" said Mungo.

"Absolutely not!" said Mum. "I'm too tired!" Because on this particular night she'd accidentally read the book **SIX TIMES** and not five!

"I'll leave the light on, if you like, so you can look at it on your own."

And so Mungo did.

But this time, it was different . . .
Oh, it was still the tale of how
Admiral Mainbrace and Nora
were **attacked** by
Barnacle Bill.

But this time, their cries for help **weren't heard**
by Captain Fleet, the bravest ship's captain of them all!

Because **Captain Fleet** was so worn out after going through the story **SIX TIMES** in one night that he'd decided to take a holiday . . .

The Seaside

. . . in Mungo's
At The Seaside book!

"MUM!"
shouted Mungo.

"Aha!"
cried Barnacle Bill.
"Now's my chance! This time, I'm going
to marry Nora the **PLUCKY** cabin girl!"

Oh no! If this went on much longer,
it wouldn't be Mungo's favourite
book any more!

"If **you** like this book so much," suggested Captain Fleet,
"why don't you do something?"
"**Me**?" gulped Mungo.
"I can't do anything!"

"Untie the girl,
me hearties,"

grinned Barnacle Bill,
"and let the wedding begin!"

"Oh, Christopher Columbus!"
cried Mungo.

Mungo shut his eyes,
held his nose
and jumped . . .

right
into
his
favourite
book!

Head over heels he tumbled and fell . . .

PLONK!

on the plank that . . .

BOINGED! like a diving board . . .

sending him somersaulting high above the ship. And down . . .

Till he landed on **Barnacle Bill**
and squished him

SPLAT!

Just like that,
flat as his hat.

"Hooray!" cried the Admiral. "We're saved!"

But he spoke too soon.

The dastardly pirates were limping towards them,
sharpening their swords and clearing their throats.

"Oh no!" yelped Mungo.

"Not the sea shanties!"

But he wasn't deterred,
for behind him he heard
the **shrieks** and the **squeaks**
of the purple **berserker bird!**

"**Aha!**" cried Mungo.
"**Now's** my **chance!**"

And he grabbed the bird so it squawked and berserked around the deck in a flurry of feathers.

The bird sent the pirates
flailing and **falling**
and **splashing**
and **sprawling!**

"Help! Help!"

they gargled and glugged.

"Don't you know
pirates can't swim?"

So Mungo and Nora
fished the pirates out of the
sea and pegged them up on
the rigging to dry.

The Admiral shook Mungo's hand.
Nora **kissed** him.

And Captain Fleet came back from his holiday.

As the Captain got ready to take his
place back in the book, he pinned
a medal on Mungo's pyjamas.
"You see what you can do
when you try," he said,
"Mr Midshipman Mungo!"

When Mungo's mum came back to turn off the light,
Mungo was fast asleep and clutching his medal,
dreaming of pirates and purple berserker birds . . .

And all the adventures that wait in
the waters off the coast of tomorrow.

The End